MW00440241

To: ———————————————

From: —————————————

(With Love)

I'd Love You Even If . . .

Annie Pigeon

Pinnacle Books

PINNACLE BOOKS are published by

Kensington Publishing Corp.
850 Third Avenue
New York, NY 10022

First Printing: February, 1996

10 9 8 7 6 5 4 3 2 1

Printed in the United States of America

For Paul and Barbara

I'd Love You Even If . . .

♥ ♥

You forgot where you hid my presents.

You told my mother what I asked you not to.

You got another parking ticket.

You forgot to tape "<u>Seinfeld.</u>"

♥ ♥

You overfed my fish.

You underwatered my plants.

You switched us to decaf without warning me.

You used one of my Elvis stamps to mail the phone bill.

♥ ♥

You temporarily misplaced your sense of humor.

You listened to rap.

You let all of our insurance lapse.

You had the laundry put starch in my pants.

You gave out my unlisted phone number.

♥ ♥

You met someone famous and didn't bring me an autograph.

You let your hair clog my drain.

You told my boss I wasn't <u>really</u> sick.

You never sent in your PBS pledge.

You woke me up during my nap.

♥ ♥

You spilled hot soup in my lap.

*You confessed your favorite Beatle
was Ringo.*

*You thought Gershwin was a kind
of pickle.*

You agreed with Rush Limbaugh.

You thought Newt was cute.

♥ ♥

♥ ♥

You went and erased my whole database.

You swept dustbunnies under the rug.

You flushed while I was taking a shower.

You invited too many houseguests.

You dented my bumper.

♥ ♥

♥ ♥

*You always needed a rest stop when
there wasn't one.*

*You borrowed my razor without
saying please.*

You left something burning on the stove.

You let the bathtub overflow.

♥ ♥

♥ ♥

*You spent my paycheck at
Banana Republic.*

You misplaced my passport.

You threw out my tax receipts.

You burned the toast.

♥ ♥

You charred the roast.

*You used my family heirloom
as a doorstop.*

*You ordered something from
an infomercial.*

You forgot to clean the kitty litter.

You undertipped.

You overpaid.

You snored all night.

You got crumbs in the sheets.

*You refused to take my calls while
"<u>Melrose Place</u>" was on.*

You stepped on my corns.

♥ ♥

You talked to yourself.

You talked to stuffed animals.

(And claimed they talked back to you.)

You let crabgrass overrun the lawn.

You forgot to floss.

♥ ♥

You rented a video I had already seen.

You forgot to rewind.

You made fun of my rock collection.

You got my CDs out of alphabetical order.

You used the last of my papaya-jojoba hair conditioner.

♥ ♥

You didn't win the lottery this week either.

You ordered anchovies.

You ate an artichoke incorrectly.

You used the wrong fork.

You mispronounced everything on the French restaurant menu.

♥ ♥

You dangled a participle.

You misspelled "potato."

You forgot to mail my letters.

You stepped on the contact lens I dropped.

You interrupted me to pick up your call waiting.

♥ ♥

You told everyone my middle name.

You promised the kids they could stay up late.

(__And__ let them eat french fries and ice cream for dinner.)

(__And__ let them watch __Aladdin__ three times in a row)

♥ ♥

♥ ♥

You joined the Hair Club for Men.

You called the Psychic Friends Network.

You forgot to pick me up at the station.

You used up all the hot water.

*You threw out everything in the fridge
that wasn't fat free.*

♥ ♥

♥ ♥

You canceled my subscription to <u>People</u>.

You screened all my calls through the answering machine.

You bought me something dainty in a size Extra Large.

You flinched when I asked to borrow your sportscar.

♥ ♥

You took too much carry-on luggage.

You fell asleep during a romantic movie.

You refused to dress up on Halloween.

*You forgot the anniversary of our
first date.*

You rooted against my home team.

You watched wrestling.

You obsessed.

You regressed.

You got a bit depressed.

You faked it.

You refused to recycle.

You cost us the bridge game.

You cheated at gin rummy.

You believed you were Marie Antoinette in a past life.

♥ ♥

You grew a goatee.

You watched Court TV.

You pierced a perfectly good body part.

You made me go shopping for antiques.

You made me spend the whole day in an outlet mall.

♥ ♥

You thought the Academy Awards were worth staying up for.

You bought creamy peanut butter instead of crunchy.

You lost my dry cleaning ticket.

You lost the house keys.

You made a wisecrack about my ancestors.

You refolded the map improperly. (And you made me use a map in the first place.)

You really liked abstract art.

You really loved progressive jazz.

♥ ♥

You took accordion lessons.

You gave accordion lessons.

You bought us tickets to see Wayne Newton.

You preferred Leno to Letterman.

You forgot to change the clocks to daylight savings time.

♥ ♥

♥ ♥

You were too scared to take that mule ride down the Grand Canyon.

You read every book about Princess Di.

You went a little nuts whenever you saw a bug.

You really liked watching mimes.

♥ ♥

You interrupted me—for a change.

You told me what you really thought of my yearbook picture.

You said something politically incorrect.

You never saved me the drumstick.

♥ ♥

You bought yellow mustard instead of Grey Poupon.

You crossed a picket line.

You lost track of time.

You wore bell-bottoms.

You took me to see the <u>Brady Bunch</u> movie.

♥ ♥

You said, "<u>Who</u> is Judge Ito?"

You only knew five state capitals.

You yelled out all the "<u>Jeopardy</u>" answers before me.

You blurted out the end of the mystery I was reading.

♥ ♥

You made me go to another stupid Super Bowl party.

You bought the chips that were fried, not baked.

You refused to ride the roller coaster with me.

You wore something made from fur.

♥ ♥

You had too many housepets.

You refused to learn how to change a tire.

You made me try to ski.

You rubbed your cold tootsies against my warm ones.

You bought a time-share vacation plan.

You pitched our tent in poison ivy.

You forgot to bring the insecticide.

You left the car windows open when it looked like rain.

You entered me in some goofy contest.

You made the waiters sing "Happy Birthday" to me.

You neglected to warn me about the surprise party.

You refused to lend me your Mastercard.

You forgot to say "<u>Gezundheit</u>."

♥ ♥

You left my umbrella in a taxi cab.

*You ran up overdue fines on my
library card.*

You bought baking soda toothpaste.

You were snippy with my best friend.

♥ ♥

You got too chummy with my best friend.

*You said I couldn't carry a tune
in a bucket.*

You broke my guitar string.

You let my bonsai die.

♥ ♥

*You believed everything in the
<u>National Enquirer</u>.*

You pointedly offered me a breath mint.

You laughed at Roadrunner cartoons.

You got lipstick stains on everything.

♥ ♥

♥ ♥

You ate the chocolate and left the vanilla.

You forgot where you parked the car.

You chewed too loud.

You refused to even <u>try</u> sushi.

♥ ♥

You refused to even <u>discuss</u> life insurance.

You enjoyed wine coolers.

You did the crossword puzzle in pen.

You played golf on our honeymoon.

You had a panic attack in Lamaze class.

You had a panic attack in the delivery room.

You had a panic attack when you saw the hospital bill.

You fell asleep and drooled on the sofa.

You blamed all our fights on PMS.

You borrowed against the retirement fund.

You dropped out of college.

You steamed open my mail.

You eavesdropped.

You ate every last corn chip in the bag.

♥ ♥

You smoked after you swore you quit.

You wiped your hands on the good guest towels.

You squeezed from the middle of the tube.

You left sour milk in the fridge.

♥ ♥

You overexposed the film.

You snapped a whole roll of pictures of your shoes.

You said, "Oh, was <u>yesterday</u> Valentine's Day?"

You left your boxers on the floor.

You forgot to lock the front door.

You never said "Excuse me."

You cooked with ingredients I was allergic to.

You had a teeny tiny tantrum.

You served margarine instead of butter.

You told everyone my secret ingredient.

♥ ♥

You overachieved.

You were a little bit ambivalent.

You said something rude about my therapist.

You said something rude <u>to</u> my therapist.

You stepped on my toes during the dance lessons.

♥ ♥

You were just a tad obsessive-compulsive.

You were just a tad anal-retentive.

You used that four letter word again.

You went to bed without apologizing.

You went to bed without letting <u>me</u> apologize.

♥ ♥

You got so stubborn you gave mules a good name.

You forgot to mention me in your will.

You went on a macrobiotic food kick.

You made me use a sugar substitute.

♥ ♥

♥ ♥ ♥ ♥ ♥ ♥ ♥ ♥ ♥ ♥ ♥ ♥ ♥ ♥ ♥ ♥ ♥ ♥ ♥ ♥

You tickled too hard.

You bit!

You sent me a belated birthday card.

You played the slot machines.

You took me a wee bit for granted.

♥ ♥ ♥ ♥ ♥ ♥ ♥ ♥ ♥ ♥ ♥ ♥ ♥ ♥ ♥ ♥ ♥ ♥ ♥ ♥

♥ ♥

You forgot to clean out the coffeepot.

You threatened to go to law school.

You left the gas tank on empty.

You hoarded the good parts of the Sunday paper.

♥ ♥

♥ ♥

You invited all our parents to dinner at the same time.

You put hot sauce on <u>everything</u>.

You chickened out on the skydive.

You thought "formal dress" meant new Reeboks.

♥ ♥

♥ ♥

You nagged.

You sagged.

You bragged.

You zigged when you should have zagged.

You forgot to RSVP.

♥ ♥

♥ ♥

You tried chewing tobacco.

You tried to improve on my recipe.

You went on a shopping spree.

You bought retail.

You threatened to throw out my old Monkees albums.

♥ ♥

♥ ♥

You signed me up to run a minimarathon.

You grew sideburns.

You exaggerated your IQ.

You fibbed about your SAT scores.

You insisted on being a matchmaker.

♥ ♥

You spread a little gossip.

You wrote fan mail to Regis and Kathie Lee.

You told a white lie.

You told an off-white lie.

You wore one black sock, one blue sock.

You shrank my favorite T-shirt.

You kept jars and jars full of pennies.

You left the TV on all night.

You sent the budget bouquet.

You said you "had a headache."

You "forgot" to throw out your little black book.

You swore you were kidnapped by an alien space race.
(And said they sent you back to get me.)

You bought me a Swatch and said it was a Rolex.

You sneaked more than ten items on the supermarket express line.

You preferred the colorized version of <u>It's A Wonderful Life</u>.

You tracked mud on the Oriental rug.

♥ ♥

You swore our kids looked just like you.

You went on a talk show and talked too much.

You turned the thermostat down after I raised it.

You kept putting off that dental checkup.

♥ ♥

You were a backseat driver.

You were a Monday morning quarterback.

You did some creative accounting and got us audited.

You signed up with the wrong long-distance phone company.

♥ ♥

You fell for a pyramid scheme.

You got my parents on <u>your</u> side.

*You said my driver's license photo
was flattering.*

*You still thought "<u>Saturday Night Live</u>"
was funny.*

♥ ♥

You said your favorite color was chartreuse.

You had a lifelong dream to own a Winnebago.

You preferred the Poconos to Tuscany.

You told everyone at the high school reunion I wasn't really a brain surgeon.

You served me a canned vegetable.

You overcooked the pasta.

You bought orange juice "made from concentrate."

You liked Yorkshire terriers.

♥ ♥

You had a pet iguana.
(And you kissed it on the lips).

You knew a shortcut that took us fifty
miles out of the way.

You got real friendly with the nosy
neighbors.

♥ ♥

♥ ♥

*The only books you read were
romance novels.*

*The only books you read were car
maintenance manuals.*

You fantasized about Madonna.

You fantasized about Fabio.

♥ ♥

You left a singing message on the answering machine.

You requested a doggie bag for your airplane meal.

You were too pooped to party.

You got carsick in my new Miata.

♥ ♥

You refused to follow doctor's orders.

*You insulted the state trooper who
pulled us over.*

You overdid it.

*You pretended to understand something
you didn't.*

You wore elevator shoes.

♥ ♥

♥ ♥

*You set the clock radio to a heavy
metal station.*

You peeked.

You tweaked.

You saw a mouse and "<u>Eeked</u>!"

♥ ♥

You washed the darks with the whites.

*You cleaned the whole house before the
cleaning lady came.*

You hoarded frequent flyer miles.

You forgot to have your shoes shined.

You forgot to have your legs waxed.

You bought too many self-help books.

You idolized Martha Stewart.

You still said "groovy."

You watched "<u>Lifestyles of the Rich and Famous</u>."

♥ ♥

You scheduled our engagement party during basketball playoffs.

You forgot to take your vitamins.

You picked up the check only at Burger King.

You interrupted my meditation.

♥ ♥

♥ ♥

You made me feel guilty.

You chewed ice.

You cracked your knuckles.

*You pretended to be asleep when
you weren't.*

You got addicted to the Weather Channel.

♥ ♥

♥ ♥

You got addicted to America Online.

You hogged the blankets.

You insisted on opening the windows in January.

You actually liked cocktail parties.

You wept when you read <u>The Bridges of Madison County</u>.

♥ ♥

You wept when you read the stock pages.

You broke all your New Year's resolutions during the Rose Bowl.

You always grabbed the window seat.

You let your mascara smear my shirt.

♥ ♥

You dropped your false eyelash in the consommé.

You said you didn't believe in Santa Claus.

You chipped my Wedgwood.

You cracked my crystal.

♥ ♥

You refused to use chopsticks.

You dozed off in church.

You gawked on the nude beach.

You mistook me for my evil twin.

You put "out" stuff in my "in" box.

You snapped a Polaroid of me when I first woke up.

You thought my older sister was my younger sister.

You commented on my overbite.

You sneezed when I brought you flowers.

*You asked me how much I spent on
your gift.*

You challenged all my Scrabble words.

You checkmated me.

*You wrote me a limerick when I asked for
a love poem.*

♥ ♥

You told the hotel clerk we weren't <u>really</u> married.

You wore a clay facial mask to bed.

You had a five o'clock shadow at two o'clock.

You were late for our rehearsal dinner.

♥ ♥

You rented a tux two sizes too large.

You channel surfed.

You watched televised golf tournaments.

You lost one of my socks whenever you did laundry.
(And stopped doing the laundry when I complained about the socks.)

♥ ♥

You used a double negative.

You hung the toilet paper backward.

You put a glass down without using a coaster.

You told your mother I wasn't perfect.

♥ ♥

♥ ♥

*You told your shrink I was a
little neurotic.*

*You only drank French mineral water,
never tap.*

You let the soufflé fall.

*You said you made the pie, when it was
really Sara Lee.*

♥ ♥

♥ ♥

You got me a gift certificate for the hardware store.

You bought me an appliance for our anniversary.

You always got the fortune cookie with the best fortune.

You went window shopping and came home with twelve windows.

♥ ♥

♥ ♥

You forgot to clean the Cuisinart.

You refused to use self-serve gasoline.

You tried to fix stuff that wasn't broken.

You ate all the cookie dough and didn't make cookies.

You took me to the movies and only got the small popcorn.

♥ ♥

♥ ♥

You once called for "Gwendolyn" in your sleep.

You claimed not to know when I was only kidding.

You stopped plucking those little hairs on your chin.

You didn't warn me about the poison sumac.

♥ ♥

♥ ♥

*You liked Woody Allen's serious films
better than his comedies.*

You had no idea where New Zealand was.

*You said, "I didn't know a whale was
a <u>mammal</u>!"*

You neglected to hold the door open for me.

You thought the baseball strike was swell.

♥ ♥

♥ ♥

You took a bite of a chocolate candy, then put it back in the box.

You took a turn in the mosh pit.

You got bifocals.

You said your favorite Olympic event was synchronized swimming.

You gave me chicken pox.

♥ ♥

♥ ♥

You left the closet doors open.

You beat me at thumb wrestling.

You sang way off-key.

You got major love handles.

You lied about your cholesterol count.

♥ ♥

♥ ♥

You had an astrological sign incompatible with mine.

You pointed out my grey hairs.

You suggested I suck in my tummy.

You said my backhand was embarrassing.

You lost at Trivial Pursuit to my nine-year-old nephew.

♥ ♥

You made me listen to <u>Tony Bennett Unplugged</u>.

You burned my favorite dinner.

You ate garlic bread in bed.

You made me watch the Learning Channel.

♥ ♥

You refused to buy anything that wasn't on sale.

You made me learn the lambada.

You said you never heard of Mozart.

You let your brother move in.

You told someone about my tummy tuck.

♥ ♥

♥ ♥

I'd love you even if you weren't the most wonderful person in the world—which you are!!!

♥ ♥